W9-BHA-235

Ciao from Rome

Written by Helen Perelman

Based on the series created by Michael Poryes and Rich Correll & Barry O'Brien

Disney PRESS

New York

Copyright © 2009 Disney Enterprises, Inc.

All rights reserved. Published by Disney Press, an imprint of Disney Book Group.
No part of this book may be reproduced or transmitted in any form or by any
means, electronic or mechanical, including photocopying, recording,
or by any information storage and retrieval system, without
written permission from the publisher. For information address
Disney Press, 114 Fifth Avenue, New York, New York 10011-5690.

Printed in the United States of America

First Edition
1 3 5 7 9 10 8 6 4 2

Library of Congress Catalog Card Number: 2008910422
ISBN 978-1-4231-1383-6

For more Disney Press fun, visit www.disneybooks.com
Visit DisneyChannel.com

Chapter One

Miley Stewart slowly sat up in bed and smiled. It was the first day of summer vacation!

Miley stretched, and jumped out of bed. As she walked down the stairs into the living room, her eyes widened. There was a large bulletin board with a world map in the middle of the room! Her dad was standing next to it with his hands on his hips.

"Hey, Daddy," Miley called tentatively, hoping he wasn't going to tell her about a

1

summer social studies class. She pointed to the large map. "What's that doing here?"

"It's your world-tour map, honey!" Robby Ray Stewart exclaimed proudly.

"*Ohhh*," Miley said, relieved.

Her dad held up red pushpins and started to put them on the map. "First stop, Rome, Italy!"

"*Ciao, Roma!*" Jackson said in an Italian accent as he entered the room. He pointed to the book he was holding, *Learn Italian Fast*. "I've been brushing up on my Italian."

"I bet," Miley said, rolling her eyes.

Jackson glared at her. Then he went over to the map and touched the red pin that indicated where Rome was. "This trip is going to be *fantastico!*" he said to his dad. He kissed the tips of his fingers and gestured like an Italian cook mixing up a delicious sauce.

Miley laughed. She had to admit that this summer *was* going to be amazing. While she loved having a normal life as Miley Stewart, she also loved being Hannah Montana, pop star. The best part was no one knew that she was Miley *and* Hannah. So she got to live like a regular teenager and a singing superstar. Now Hannah Montana was going to go international, and she couldn't wait!

The tour included all the hot spots around the globe—from Australia to Brazil.

When he finished marking all the cities on the map, Mr. Stewart put his arm around his daughter. "This *is* going to be a fantastic summer, Mile! Rome is the perfect place to start the tour. There's so much to see and do!" He gestured to the stack of guidebooks on the coffee table. "I can't wait to see the Colosseum and the Pantheon and the Piazza di Spagna!"

"Piazza di Spagna?" Jackson said, making a face. "Is that like a spinach pizza?"

"No, noodlehead," Miley said, giving

Jackson a playful slap. "That's the Spanish Steps—a famous spot in Rome. There's a large town square with all these steps that's great for people watching."

Mr. Stewart raised an eyebrow. "How'd you know that?" he asked.

"Dad, you're not the only one reading all those guidebooks," Miley confessed. She grinned, tossing her long brown hair over her shoulder. "Don't get me wrong, I want to visit all the clothing and shoe stores, but there's a lot of cool stuff to see in Rome besides that. I can't wait to have espresso in a street café!"

"You better take the espresso lane up those stairs and get to packing if you want to go to any Italian cafés," Mr. Stewart told her. "Roxy will be here soon, and then we'll head over to the airport. She's nervous about the crowds, so we're going extra-early."

Roxy was Hannah Montana's bodyguard.

Her job was to keep Hannah safe, and she took it seriously.

"First class, baby!" Jackson said, doing a little dance. "I can't wait for the snacks on the private jet." He rubbed his stomach. "I wonder if they'll have nachos."

Miley stared at him. "Is food all you think about?"

Jackson smirked. "No. I also like to ponder monster trucks and comics." He paused. "Italian food is one of my favorites."

"Me, too," Mr. Stewart said, with a far-off look in his eye. "I can't wait for a huge bowl of spaghetti and some old-fashioned meat sauce. *Mmmm*, I can almost taste it now!"

Miley picked up a guidebook. "Did you know that Italian leather is among the finest in the world?" She looked at her brother and father. "Especially their boots," she added.

Mr. Stewart shot her a look.

"C'mon, Dad," Miley said. "How great

would it be to kick off my world tour in an awesome new pair of leather boots?"

"We'll see," her father said. "First, we've got to get there."

"I'm almost packed," Miley said.

"She's taking an empty suitcase," Jackson said.

Mr. Stewart gave his daughter a stern look. "Miley?"

"I'm just leaving room for any accessories that I might come across," Miley said.

"Since you've got more skirts in your Hannah closet than you know what do with, I suggest that you go upstairs and pack some of them," her dad replied.

Miley shrugged. "Fine," she said as she started up the stairs. "But I'll take an extra duffel bag, just in case." She paused and turned around, an excited look on her face. "Watch out, world, Hannah Montana is coming!"

Chapter Two

"Are you ready?" Roxy asked an hour later.

Miley nodded. She knew the drill. As soon as she stepped out of the limo, she would pose for a few photos. Then she'd move quickly through airport security. Roxy had told the airport staff about Hannah Montana's flight, so everyone was prepared.

"Let's do this!" Miley said. She straightened her blond Hannah Montana wig and got ready. Once the door was open, she was no longer Miley Stewart, ordinary teenager. She was Hannah Montana, superstar! She grabbed her bag. It was filled with magazines for the plane ride, her iPod, and a travel journal that Lilly had given her before she left. It had been hard to say good-bye to her best friends, but Lilly and Oliver had made a deal that they would meet up with her at some point during the summer. Having friends around always made things much more fun.

Mr. Stewart gave Miley a nod. He was dressed in his secret identity, too. Just as Miley put on a wig when she was Hannah Montana, her dad wore a fake mustache and a hat when he was Hannah Montana's manager. He opened the limo door, and immediately, flashbulb lights popped and reporters began to call out questions.

"Hannah! This way!"

"Are you excited about your world tour?"

one reporter asked as soon as Hannah slid out of the car.

"You bet!" Miley said with a grin. She stood and smiled for the photographers.

"Have you ever been to Rome?" a young woman asked.

"No," Miley said. "I am so excited that Rome is the first city on the tour. I'm really looking forward to seeing my fans all over the world. We've got a great show planned for them."

More flashbulbs sparked.

"Okay, let's keep moving," Roxy said in her ear. She steered Miley through crowds hoping to glimpse their favorite singer.

"The flight is on time," her dad said as he checked the large information board.

Roxy got Hannah through the airport security checkpoints. There were still a couple left. Being a celebrity didn't get her out of all the lines. But with Roxy at her side, no one bothered her as she walked through the crowded airport. People just pointed and snapped photos. Finally, they arrived at the gate and boarded the plane.

The luxury plane didn't have a crowd of people boarding. The only passengers besides Hannah were her dad, Jackson, Roxy, and two attendants, ready to serve food and snacks. There were no rows of seats like in a commercial airplane. Instead, there were four leather couches facing a large television and a long table with two leather benches. A fuzzy beige carpet covered the floor.

"It's like a living room in the sky!" Jackson said as Miley stepped onto the plane. He was sitting on the couch with a bowl of popcorn.

Jackson had been announced as the winner of a superfan contest that meant he got all kinds of prizes, including traveling with Hannah Montana to all of the stops on her world tour. It was the perfect way to explain why he was always with Hannah!

Miley glanced at the television and groaned. Her brother already had a monster-truck video playing.

"Hey, Jackson," she said, "I think there are nachos over by the table."

"Really?" he said eagerly.

Miley pulled a DVD out of the cabinet by the television and popped it in the machine. There was no way she was watching giant trucks on her way to Italy.

Roxy set herself up at the long table with her maps and her laptop.

"Roxy," Mr. Stewart said, "what are you doing?"

Smiling, Roxy smoothed out the map in front of her. "I am planning my Italian gelato tour," she explained. "Gelato is my favorite Italian food, and I plan to sample it at all the best places. We don't have a lot of time, so I need to be strategic about my trip to ice-cream heaven."

"Sounds like a good plan," Miley said. She glanced over Roxy's shoulder at the high-lighted maps and charts. "Count me in."

At that moment, all Miley wanted to do was curl up on the soft couch and chill out, but she knew that she had to keep wearing her wig and pretend to be Hannah for the airline attendants. Miley Stewart wasn't going on tour, Hannah Montana was!

"My niece loves you," the flight attendant with dark hair cooed. "I'm not supposed to ask, but it would mean so much to her if you would sign this." The woman held out a small white napkin.

Hannah was used to those kinds of requests.

"We'll be taking off in a few minutes," the attendant said after Hannah autographed the napkin. "Please take a seat on one of the couches and buckle up. We are next in line for takeoff."

"I can't find the nachos, but this is the greatest!" Jackson said. "I'm never going back to regular airlines again!"

"Easy, high roller," his father cautioned. "Don't get so used to this." He sat down on the extrasoft couch and stretched out his long legs. "Ah, but this is a nice way to travel!"

"You know it!" Hannah cheered. She popped in her earpieces and began listening to the playlist that Lilly had made for her. The music made her happy. From her bag, she took out the sheet of paper that Lilly had also given her before she left. Her best friend had researched all the best stores in Rome so Miley could check them out. Especially the leather-shoe stores.

The engines roared, and the plane began to gain speed as it zoomed down the runway. Miley shut her eyes and felt the wheels lift off the ground. *Eee, doggies!* Her trip around the world had officially begun.

Chapter Three

"Ms. Montana, we will be arriving in Rome shortly," the flight attendant said. She gently shook Miley's shoulder. "You'll need to fasten your seat belt, please."

Miley stretched. She reached for her seat belt. She didn't remember falling asleep, but she was glad that she had. Now she was rested and ready to roam through Rome!

She looked over to see her dad and Jackson standing by a large window on the side of the aircraft.

"Can you see anything?" she asked.

"Just some tiny dots," Jackson replied, squinting.

"Please, take your seats," the attendant told them. "We all need to be seated for landing."

Miley's dad and Jackson went back to their seats. Roxy walked over and sat down next to Miley. "Remember the ground rules for this tour," she said. "You must never leave my side. You must never leave my sight. You must never leave me!"

Miley laughed. "I got it," she said. "I promise to be safe. I'll be especially good if you can lead me to one of those gelato places!"

"Sweet deal!" Roxy said, giving Miley a high five.

There were several reporters waiting for Hannah Montana at the gate in Rome. Thanks to her large sunglasses and wide-brimmed hat, Miley wasn't stopped. But right before she got to the exit, someone recognized her.

"There's Hannah Montana!" a little girl screamed.

Suddenly, a large crowd gathered. At times like these, Miley was glad that she had a bodyguard!

Roxy swiftly got her to the limousine. When the door closed, Miley took a deep breath.

"Everyone okay?" Mr. Stewart asked.

"Just exhausted," Miley said. "But happy we're here!"

Her dad gazed out the window. "We'll head to the hotel so we can clean up," he said. "I want to hit a few sights before dinner tonight." He clapped his hands together, eager to get rolling.

After a few minutes, the limo pulled up to a beautiful old hotel. Miley thought the place looked like a castle. The hotel staff was at the front door to greet them.

"*Benvenuta, signorina!* Welcome, Ms. Montana!" said a man dressed in a very fancy hotel uniform. "I am Roberto, the manager here. We are very happy to have you stay with us. *Prego*, please, let us know if there is anything that we can do to make your stay more pleasurable."

"*Grazie*, thank you," Miley said, smiling. Everyone was so nice! Roberto smiled broadly when Miley answered in Italian. It was a good thing Jackson had bought that *Learn Italian Fast* book!

Roxy directed Miley toward the elevator before anyone noticed her.

"This place is unbelievable!" Jackson exclaimed when he walked into the hotel suite. The main room of the suite was bigger than their living room at home.

"Ya think?" Miley said, gazing at the plush rugs and sparkling crystal chandelier.

"Did you know that part of the hotel

17

was actually built in the eighteenth century?" Mr. Stewart said, looking around. "They certainly know how to upgrade here." He turned back to his kids. "Everyone has their own bathroom, so let's all get cleaned up and go sightseeing. As Uncle Earl likes to say, 'When I get my sights set on seeing things, I like to move quicker than a bird dog hot on the trail.'"

Miley rolled her eyes. Then she went into her room. She figured she had a different idea of how to tour the city than he did, but a nice hot shower did seem like a perfect plan.

A little while later, everyone was ready. Miley carefully put her Hannah wig in her suitcase. She was looking forward to quietly exploring the city without any reporters trailing after her.

But after one look at her dad, she knew that everyone would be staring at her if she were anywhere near him. With a baseball hat, a fanny pack, a camera hanging from his neck, and sunglasses, he looked like a typical tourist.

"Dad!" Miley exclaimed as she walked into the main room of the suite. "What are you thinking?"

"I'm thinking that we have a lot of ground to cover so we better leave soon." He slapped the brochure in his hand. "So much to see, so little time."

Jackson gasped when he walked into the room. He shielded his eyes as if he were looking directly into the sun. "So hard to take!"

Mr. Stewart didn't pay attention to his children. He went over to the table to get his map. When he turned around, they were still staring.

"Ready to go?" he asked.

"Uh . . . I think I'll go with Roxy today," Miley replied.

19

"Me, too," Jackson quickly added.

Mr. Stewart looked at them closely. "Stick together and stay close to Roxy," he warned. "Tomorrow night is the concert, so you'll need to come back early this evening. Even though we got some shut-eye on the plane, jet lag is going to set in soon."

"I don't get affected by jet lag!" Roxy cried. She stuck out her chest proudly. "Okay, who's ready for some gelato?"

"I gotta get me a lotta gelato!" Jackson piped up.

"I've got a special ride for us down-stairs," Roxy told them. "There's a saying, 'when in Rome, do as the Romans do,' and that's what we're going to do!"

Mr. Stewart raised an eyebrow.

"I mean that I got us a couple of motor scooters to drive around town on!" Roxy explained. "One for Jackson, and one for Miley and me to share." She smiled proudly.

"Sweet sausages!" Jackson cried. "That's awesome, Roxy. This is going to be great."

"Can I drive?" Miley asked, hopeful.

Roxy shook her head. "That's a negative," she said.

"Anyone want to head over to the Pantheon?" Mr. Stewart asked. "It's one of the oldest parts of Rome—even older than Great-aunt Delilah."

"And you'll take lots of pictures of it, I'm sure," Jackson said, kidding his dad.

"All right," Mr. Stewart said, realizing that he wasn't going to get his kids to go with him. "Be safe. I'll see you back here later for dinner. Roberto is tracking down the city's best spaghetti for us."

"We love Roberto!" Jackson cheered.

"We love Rome!" Miley said, grinning. "Let's go!"

Chapter Four

From the back of Roxy's scooter, Miley took in all the sights and smells of Rome. And all the cool shoes the Italians were wearing.

Roxy was weaving in and out of traffic, eager to get to the first stop on her gelato tour.

"It should be up there on the left," Roxy said, pointing. She motioned to Jackson, who was on a scooter right behind them.

Then they saw it—a large *gelateria* on the corner. Miley and Roxy hopped off their scooters and peered inside. Two long cases were filled with the icy dessert in every color imaginable. Miley glanced at Roxy.

"It's just as I pictured it!" Roxy said.

"Ah, wait until you taste the gelato!" a woman who was walking out of the shop said. "It's wonderful!"

"What are we waiting for?" Jackson asked. "Isn't it time to eat?"

Roxy locked up the scooters. "Let's go."

Miley and Jackson followed Roxy inside the shop. On little cards above the tubs of gelato, there were pictures of the flavors with their Italian names. Roxy had her guidebook out. She had come prepared.

"*Ciao!*" Roxy said to the man behind the counter. "*Un cono con due gusti, per favore.*"

"Sweet niblets!" Jackson exclaimed. "You're practically fluent. Have you been reading my *Learn Italian Fast* book?"

Roxy smiled. "I like to study the situation

23

and be prepared. I ordered a cone with two scoops." She rubbed her hands together. "Now, it's time for the flavor." She walked the length of the counter three times. "*Lampone e cioccolato fondente, per favore*," she said to the man behind the counter. When he handed her the cone, she said, "*Grazie!*"

"Hey, what did you order?" Jackson asked.

"The house special," Roxy replied. "A scoop of raspberry and a scoop of dark chocolate. *Mmmmmmm!*" She closed her eyes as she tried the gelato.

Miley studied the pictures on the labels and then tried her best to pronounce the one with chocolate chips. When the man behind the counter looked at her with a questioning expression, Roxy came to her rescue.

"*Stracciatella*," Roxy told her. You say it like, *strah-cha-TEL-lah*."

The man grinned and made Miley her cone.

"And what about this one?" Jackson asked, pointing to the tub with a strawberry on the label.

"Strawberry is *fragola*. You say *frah-go-lah*," Roxy instructed.

"Cool," Jackson said as the man handed him a strawberry cone. "I mean, *grazie*!" he said, nodding at the man.

Once the three of them had their cones, they walked to the piazza across the street.

Miley pointed straight ahead. "There are the Spanish Steps!" she cried. "Just like in the guidebook!" She looked at all the people hanging out on the steps. Some were reading, some were chatting with friends, and some were looking for friends! "This is so great! Let's go sit," she said, pulling Roxy along.

"Hey, wait!" Jackson said. A small kiosk with magazines and comic books caught his eye. He stopped to take a look. "They have the latest *Mighty Brinito*!" Jackson exclaimed.

"Oh, brother," Miley said, sighing. She stood with her hands on her hips. She could tell that Jackson was about to get all goofy about his comic-book obsession.

"I can get the newest one right now!" Jackson said. He was jumping up and down with excitement.

Miley wanted to hide. Her brother was so embarrassing!

Suddenly, Jackson stopped jumping. He had opened the comic book to the first page. "Oh, no," he moaned. "This is all in Italian! I can't read Italian!

"Hey Roxy," he said. "Can you translate it?"

"Sorry," Roxy replied. "I only studied gelato-related words."

Patting him on the back, Miley tried to be sympathetic. "At least you'll be the first one at home to have this," she said. "You can look at the pictures."

Jackson wasn't listening, though. He was

off in another corner of the kiosk. "And look at these!" he said. He reached over to grab another stack of comic books.

Miley shook her head. "Oh, no," she said. She had seen that look in Jackson's eyes before. He was going to want to stay and look at those comics for a long, long time. She glanced over at Roxy. "How about we just meet up with Captain Jackson-o later?" she asked.

"Jackson, we'll be over on the far left of those steps, okay?" Roxy said to him. She pointed toward the crowded steps. "And if we get separated, you know my cell number."

Jackson waved Roxy on. His head was already buried in another comic book.

Miley climbed to the top of the steps so she could get a good view. She wanted to do some people watching! She'd have to snap a few photos to send to Lilly and Oliver.

Roxy sat down next to her. "I'd like to

finish my gelato," she said. Then she smiled. "And try another from the shop over there."

Sure enough, there was another gelato shop. "Is it okay if I stay here while you go?" Miley asked. She watched Roxy's face carefully. "I'll be fine, really. I just want to sit here on the steps and watch the scene. Besides, Jackson should be along soon."

Roxy scanned the crowd and looked back at Miley. "I guess it's okay," she said. "But keep your cell phone on—and don't move!"

"I promise," Miley said. She took out her cell phone and texted Lilly. She had to tell her how cool Rome was! But when she finished, Jackson was nowhere in sight. Miley had a feeling that he hadn't listened to what Roxy had said. Her eyes scanned the crowd. Was Jackson lost in Rome?

Chapter Five

*J*ackson walked away from the third kiosk he had visited that afternoon, grinning. In his hand, he had the newest *Mighty Brinito* and two other comic books. He could figure out most of the story from the pictures. And back at the hotel, he knew that his dad had an Italian-to-English dictionary. Jackson could translate the story!

Just as he was about to head back to the hotel, Jackson realized that he had no idea where Miley and Roxy had gone. He remembered Roxy had told him something, but he had been too busy checking out comics to listen. There were so many people walking around the piazza. He would never find them! Where had Roxy said they'd be? He scratched his head. Just then, his cell phone rang.

"*Pronto*!" he said into the phone. He had heard a few Italians answer their cell phones that way. He wanted to sound Italian.

"Jackson, is that you?" Miley asked.

"Where are you?" Jackson replied.

"Don't you remember that we said we'd meet you at the Spanish Steps on the left?" Miley blurted out.

"Hmmm," Jackson said. "Not really. Sorry. I'm going to get the scooter and head back to the hotel. Tell Roxy, okay?"

"Sure," Miley said. "She's getting more gelato. I'm hanging out on the steps. This place is the coolest!"

"See you later," Jackson said. "I mean, *ciao*!"

Miley ended the call and went back to her people watching. A girl who appeared to be around the same age as Miley walked by. She was wearing a blue leather hat and a funky pink sweater jacket. Lilly would love a hat just like that, Miley thought to herself. She stood up.

"Excuse me," Miley said sweetly. "Do you speak English?"

"*Si*, I mean, yes," the girl answered. She had large brown eyes and a friendly smile. "Are you lost? Do you need directions?"

"Oh, I'm not lost," Miley said. "I was wondering where I could get a hat like yours. My best friend at home would love it!"

The girl smiled. "This is from one of my favorite stores. I can show you where it is. It's right over there, next to the *gelateria*."

Miley nodded. Perfect, she thought. She

could run in and tell Roxy that she was going to the store next door. "I'm Miley," she said, holding out her hand. She smiled at the girl.

"I'm Daniella," the girl told her. "Are you visiting from the United States?"

Miley blushed. "Yes, I am. You could tell right away from my accent, huh?"

Daniella smiled warmly. "Yes, and welcome to Rome!" She started to walk down the steps. "Follow me," she instructed. "The store is just over there."

As Miley followed Daniella, she hummed a song. She was so excited! Just as she had expected, there were so many cool accessories and clothes in Rome. And now she had a chance to buy something for Lilly!

When the two girls got to the bottom of the steps, Daniella pointed to the shop. "Here it is," she said. "It's called *Fiore*. That means 'flower' in Italian."

At that moment, Roxy walked out of the

gelato shop and smiled at Miley. She held out her cone. "You have to taste this cinnamon. It's heaven!"

Miley shook her head. Cinnamon ice cream didn't sound so good to her. "Roxy, this is Daniella," she said, introducing her new friend. "We're going into this shop, okay?"

"Hmmm," Roxy said. "Remember that you need to stay close."

"I know," Miley said. "Jackson went back to the hotel already. But I want to check out this store. Wouldn't Lilly love this hat?" She pointed to Daniella's head.

Roxy just nodded. She was focused on her gelato. "I'll be right here," she said, pointing to a bench.

Inside the store, Miley's eyes grew wide with excitement. There were leather jackets, leather boots, leather gloves, and leather hats, even leather barrettes! There were so many

33

colors, too, not just brown and black. Miley couldn't help but smile.

"It *is* a great store," Daniella said, watching her new friend take in the scene. "Here, this is the hat that I am wearing. Do you think your friend would like the purple one or the blue one?"

Miley picked up the hat that Daniella was holding. She thought of Lilly and immediately knew the answer. "She'd like the blue one," Miley said. Then her eyes flew to the tall black boots up on the wall. "And I would *love* those!"

A saleswoman walked over and spoke very quickly in Italian. Miley just stared at her. She had no idea what the woman was saying!

Thankfully, Daniella answered for her.

"She wants to know if you would like to try those on," Daniella said. "I told her you would." She smiled at Miley. "Was that the right answer?"

"Oh, yes!" Miley said. "I would love to wear them tomorrow night."

"You have a big date?" Daniella asked, grinning.

Miley giggled. "No," she said. "I'm doing some sightseeing with my dad," she added, not wanting to mention the concert.

Daniella nodded. "You still need to wear shoes!"

The girls sat on the couch while the saleswoman went to get the boots.

"Thanks for bringing me here," Miley told her new friend.

"I'm glad that I could," Daniella said. "I love this place. And they definitely have the best stuff."

"Do you live here in the city?" Miley asked.

Daniella nodded. "Yes," she said. "I live with my parents and my older sister. I've never lived anywhere else!"

The woman appeared with the boots.

Miley slipped off her shoes and put them on.

"*Perfecto!*" the saleswoman exclaimed.

"They look great on you," Daniella confirmed.

Miley walked over to the large mirror on the wall. The boots almost came up to her knees, and they looked amazing. Wow, thought Miley. These would be great for the Hannah world tour! They'd be perfect for the final number. She just had to get them.

"I'll take 'em!" she said, smiling broadly.

"Excellent!" the saleswoman cheered.

Daniella clapped her hands together. "I love them on you!"

"I look Italian, huh?" Miley said, winking.

"*Si, signorina!*" Daniella said with a giggle.

After she bought the boots, and the hat for Lilly, the two new friends walked outside.

"This was fun," Daniella said. "Will you be staying in Rome long?"

Miley shook her head. "We're only here a

couple of days. Maybe we could hang out tomorrow afternoon?"

"Sounds good," Daniella replied. "Would you like to go to my favorite *gelateria*?"

Roxy jumped up from her seat on a nearby bench. She already liked Miley's new friend! *"Perfecto!"* Roxy exclaimed.

Miley laughed. "Daniella, this is Roxy. She is watching out for me while I'm here in Rome. She's also a little bit obsessed with gelato, so you just became her best friend!"

Daniella grinned. "Gelato is a good thing! Don't worry, Roxy. I'll show you a great place tomorrow."

"A la Piazza di Spagna?" Miley asked. She was trying out her Italian. She was happy when Daniella nodded.

"Yes, at the Spanish Steps tomorrow," Daniella agreed. "At two?"

"Si," Miley said. *"Ciao!"* Being in Rome was so much fun!

Chapter Six

The next morning there was a rehearsal for the Hannah Montana concert. Miley wore her new boots. It felt great to dance onstage in stylish Italian leather boots!

After the rehearsal, Miley had changed out of her Hannah outfit and was packing a bag in her dressing room when her father knocked on the door. "Hey, bud," he greeted her. Jackson was right behind him, but he didn't say a word. His nose was in one of his new comic books.

"You sounded great!" her dad said as he gave her a big hug. "Being on tour is good for you, huh?"

Miley agreed. There were a couple of new songs that she was trying out on the tour. The new music was fun and fresh, and she was having a good time. She especially liked the new dance routines created for the show. The concert was going to be a good one!

"Now that the rehearsal is over, anyone want to check out the Sistine Chapel?" Mr. Stewart asked hopefully. "What do you say? A little tour time?"

Jackson didn't even look up from his comic book. In one hand he had a pocket dictionary, and in the other he had the comic book. "No can do," he said. He pointed to the page. "Mighty Brinito is about to save the planet!"

Mr. Stewart shrugged. He glanced over at Miley. "What do you say?"

"Daddy, I'd love to," Miley said sweetly.

Her father's face lit up.

"But . . ." Miley sang out. "I already made plans with Daniella. We're going to meet up at the Spanish Steps. Sorry!"

With a sigh, Mr. Stewart grabbed his camera and his guidebooks. "Stay close to Roxy," he ordered. "And remember, no more shopping in expensive Italian stores!"

"Don't worry, Daddy," Miley said, smiling. "I'll be good."

Her father gave her a kiss on the check. "Okay," Mr. Stewart said, "I'm going to drop some things at the hotel and go. I'll see you later."

"You got it," Miley told her dad. "I'm so psyched for the concert tonight! I've got new numbers *and* new boots!" She flashed her dad a huge smile and winked.

Roxy was waiting outside at the stage door. She was sitting on the scooter. Her large, dark sunglasses covered much of her face. "Ready?" she called out when she saw Miley walk outside.

"*Sì!*" Miley said. After rehearsal, she was glad to take off her Hannah Montana wig and get back to just being Miley. Plus, she was excited to hang out with her new Italian friend.

"Hold on!" Roxy shouted. She started up the motor on the small scooter, and they zoomed off through the busy streets of Rome.

When they got to the Spanish Steps, Daniella was waiting.

"Hello!" Daniella exclaimed. "How are you?"

"Great!" Miley said. She was very happy to see her friend.

"Hello, Roxy!" Daniella said. "You can follow me. I parked my scooter over there." She pointed to a red scooter a few feet away. "The place isn't far."

Miley hung on tight as Roxy followed

Daniella through narrow side streets. She loved seeing the shops along the way and all the people hanging out in the cafés.

The *gelateria* that Daniella had been talking about was on a narrow street. It wasn't as flashy and bright as the ones from the day before, but the gelato looked really good. "My friend's *nonna*, her grandmother, makes the gelato here," Daniella explained. "It's the best!"

"*Hmmm*," Roxy said as she walked in. She inspected the store and walked up and down the long counter.

"It's going to take her a long time to order," Miley whispered to Daniella. "Let's get our gelato and grab a seat outside. I totally want to people watch!"

Daniella laughed. "Oh, this is a great spot for people watching! I love that you like to do that, too!"

The girls found a seat at the end of the

row of tables outside. The sun was bright and everyone had their sunglasses on. Not only was the gelato delicious, the place was beautiful!

"Where do you live in the United States?" Daniella asked.

"California," Miley told her. "It's pretty different from Rome. I live near the beach. We don't have old buildings like you do here." Then she noticed someone at the next table. "Everyone is so fashionable. I mean, how cool is that girl's shirt?"

"Thank you!" the girl said in English. She turned to look at Miley.

Miley felt her face grow bright red. She hadn't thought that the girl would hear her! She was so embarrassed! It was one thing to people watch—it was another to get caught!

"It's a Nicola Umberto original," the girl continued. "She's a new designer. Her show-room is just around the corner."

A showroom of an Italian designer? Miley's heart started to pound faster and faster. How cool was that? She had read about European showrooms in magazines, but she had never been to an Italian one! She knew that her dad said no more shopping in expensive stores, but he hadn't said anything about dropping by a designer's showroom!

"What do you think?" Miley asked Daniella. From the look on Daniella's face, she knew that her new friend was just as excited.

Miley was going to meet a real Italian fashion designer! She couldn't wait to tell Lilly!

"If the building is just around the corner, let's go find it," Daniella said.

"Let me just tell Roxy," Miley responded. "I'm sure she hasn't finished ordering her gelato yet."

Sure enough, when Miley walked back into the *gelateria*, Roxy was still pacing in front of the counter.

"There are too many choices," Roxy said when she saw Miley. "But I think I've finally narrowed them down. I'm going to get five scoops today. I just have to!"

Miley laughed. "Great," she said. "Enjoy. I'm going to head over to a designer showroom around the corner. Don't worry, I have my cell. Okay?"

"Hmmm, good," Roxy said. Then she narrowed her eyes and gave Miley a long look. "Be on your toes. And keep that cell phone close."

"You got it!" Miley said. She held up her phone. "I'm connected, I promise!"

Miley rushed outside. She wondered if Nicola Umberto had any more shirts like the one Miley had admired. A long shirt like that would look amazing with leggings—and her new tall leather boots!

Chapter Seven

Miley could hardly wait to visit a real Italian showroom. As she walked down the street with Daniella, she smiled. Being on a world tour was amazing, but hanging out with someone like Daniella and meeting a fashion designer made it even better!

"Over there you can see a bit of the Colosseum," Daniella said. She pointed over Miley's head. "Have you been there yet?"

"No," Miley said. "My dad and I might go see it together. My history teacher said that it

Fantastico! It's the perfect outfit for Hannah's second set.

Jackson is psyched that he found the new
Mighty Brinito comic book!

Miley and Mr. Stewart can't wait to visit the Colosseum.

Ready to rock the stage in Rome!

was the ultimate concert hall of its day!"

Daniella laughed. "Yes, that's true. There's a ton of history here in Rome. My *nonna* will talk forever about the city. She used to be a tour guide."

"Well, we should introduce her to my supertourist dad," Miley said, laughing. "They'd be perfect for each other."

As the girls giggled, Miley walked right into Jackson. He was reading the *Mighty Brinito* comic as he walked along the street.

"Hey, noodlehead!" Miley shouted. "Watch where you're going!" Then she considered how strange it was to bump into him on the street in a big city like Rome. She glared at him. "Did Dad send you to spy on me?"

Jackson looked at her innocently. "No, I'm just looking for another kiosk. Roberto at the hotel told me that there's one around here that sells *Mighty Brinito* comics."

Miley shook her head. She was about to say something but realized that Daniella was standing there waiting for an introduction.

"Daniella, this is my brother, Jackson," Miley said. She hoped that he wouldn't embarrass her, but she knew it was really only a matter of time, especially because of his obsession with the Italian comic book.

"Is that the new *Mighty Brinito*?" Daniella asked. She looked over at the comic in Jackson's hands.

Oh, no, thought Miley. Here it comes! Jackson is going to spit out everything he knows about his favorite superhero!

"Yes," Jackson said proudly. He turned the comic around so Daniella could see the cover. "I just got the newest one yesterday."

Daniella smiled. "Oh, can I see?" She reached out for the comic book. "I love the Mighty Brinito!"

Miley couldn't believe her ears! Daniella

liked comic books? More unbelievable than that, Daniella seemed more than happy to talk to Jackson about the little man in the purple and orange outfit flying through the pages of the book!

"Um, Jackson," Miley said, looking at her watch. "I hate to break up this comic chat, but we were on our way to see a fashion designer."

Normally the word *fashion* made Jackson break out in hives and run for cover. He hated shopping. Miley often wondered how they could be related!

"Yes, why don't you come with us?" Daniella asked. She looked up at Jackson with her large brown eyes.

Miley's mouth dropped open. Could it be that Daniella was actually enjoying talking to Jackson? Maybe she wasn't just being nice. Maybe she really did like the Mighty Brinito—and Jackson!

"Sure," Jackson said. His face blushed a

deep shade of red. "I'd love to come along." He turned and smirked at Miley.

On the next block, they saw a tall square building with large windows.

"This is it," Daniella exclaimed. "We need to go to the third floor."

"This is so exciting!" Miley squealed.

Jackson rushed to hold the door open for Daniella.

Wow, thought Miley. She was actually impressed, until Jackson followed Daniella in. The door closed just as Miley was about to go through it. I guess pea brain only has enough manners to impress one person, Miley thought.

When the elevator doors opened on the third floor, there was a tall man standing in front of two closed red doors.

"You need to wait here," the man said. He spoke in a heavy accent. "No one gets in without my okay." He stood with his arms folded against his chest.

"Yikes," Miley said. She had heard of tight security around designers, but this guy seemed a bit too serious.

"Maybe we should just wait here a little," Daniella offered. "The girl said that Nicola was really nice. Maybe she'll let us in."

There were two long couches set against the wall. Miley, Daniella, and Jackson sat down and tried to wait patiently.

Just then, the elevator doors opened. A crowd of people walked out. In the center was a tall, beautiful model. Miley recognized her from a magazine that she had read on the airplane. The model had curly brown hair and large almond-shaped eyes.

"Wow." Daniella sighed. "I know who that is!" she whispered to Miley.

"I've seen her photos," Miley said. "She had a huge spread in the magazine that I just read. She's gorgeous."

"She goes by V," Daniella whispered. "I'm not sure if that is short for anything."

"Hmmm," Jackson said. He was watching the guard at the door. "I think Muscleman over there likes her. He's opening the door for her."

V walked straight into the showroom. Muscleman didn't ask her any questions. He just smiled and nodded. "Welcome," he said.

"It must be nice to be famous and get in wherever you want," Daniella whispered.

Miley looked over at Jackson. A quick change into Hannah Montana would solve all this!

"You know what?" Miley said, trying to sound very casual. "I think I better go check on Roxy." She motioned for Jackson to follow her. "Don't worry, Daniella," Miley told her friend. "I have a feeling that we'll get in to the showroom very soon."

Jackson handed his comic book to

Daniella and walked toward Miley.

"I'm okay waiting here," Daniella said. "Especially if Jackson lets me read this!"

"You stay here," Miley whispered to Jackson. "I'm going back to the hotel with Roxy. I think Hannah Montana might want to do a little shopping. Could you please try not to do anything weird? Daniella is my friend, and I don't want to come back and find her gone."

"Relax, sis," Jackson said. "The Italian ladies are like putty in my hands." Then he began to strut over toward Daniella. *"Ciao,"* he called to Miley, turning his head. But he hadn't noticed the potted plant by the elevator. He tripped over it and fell on the floor.

Daniella giggled while Jackson grinned sheepishly.

"Oh, brother," Miley said. She hoped her plan worked . . . before Jackson tried to impress Daniella again!

Chapter Eight

M iley raced back to the *gelateria*. Roxy was sitting outside enjoying a bowl of colorful gelato.

"Hi, Roxy," Miley called as she walked up to the small café table.

When Roxy saw Miley alone, she jumped out of her seat. "What's the situation?" Immediately, she sensed that something was up. She leaped into a karate-fighting pose. Her dark eyes darted around the area. "What's going on? Any trouble? What happened?" She held her hands up in the air, ready for action.

Laughing, Miley shook her head. "Relax— no international incident," she told Roxy. "At least not yet." She thought of Jackson alone with Daniella and Muscleman.

"I need to get back to the hotel for a quick change," Miley explained. "You can stay here, and I'll just scoot back myself." Miley gave Roxy a pleading look.

Roxy didn't fall for it. At all. "No dice," she replied. Standing up, she pushed back her chair. She shoved a couple of spoonfuls of gelato into her mouth. She wasn't about to let it go to waste! "I'll drive you back," she said. "We'll be there in a flash. Roxy guaranteed."

Miley couldn't argue with that—she didn't have time! Quickly, they zoomed back to the hotel. Miley changed into her Hannah wig and then stood in front of her open suitcase. What should Hannah wear to a designer's showroom? There wasn't a whole lot of time to waste, but she wanted to make the right decision. In this situation, basic seemed best. She pulled a black sweater and some new jeans out of the suitcase.

Once she was inside the showroom, she'd be able to talk to Nicola. Hannah could put in a good word for her friends waiting outside. After a quick change back to plain old Miley, they'd all get to go in. This way Daniella would get a chance to experience the thrill of hanging out with a designer.

"So is Hannah Montana hitting the many sights of Rome?" Mr. Stewart asked. He stood in the doorway and gave his daughter a quizzical look. He was surprised to see her dressed as Hannah so many hours before the concert.

Miley didn't move. She hadn't planned on bumping into her dad while she was doing her quick change.

"Uh, sort of," Miley said quickly.

"I was just about to leave for the Sistine Chapel. Want to come?" Mr. Stewart said.

"I can't. I'm trying to do something nice for Daniella, so I've got to get going."

Miley's father smiled wistfully. "I was hoping we'd get some time to see the sights together, Mile. Your mama would be so proud to see you on tour in Europe. She always wanted to come to Italy."

Miley went to her dad. "Thanks, Daddy." She smiled at him. "Let's go sightseeing in the morning, just you and me. Maybe we can get some of that espresso."

"I bet it won't hold a candle to my *loco* hot cocoa," her father said, winking. "Now git. You've got stuff to do and a little ole concert to put on tonight. Don't be late."

"I won't. Promise. See ya!" With that, Miley raced out of the suite.

Outside, Roxy was waiting on the scooter.

"Ready to get back to gelato and high fashion?" Miley asked.

Roxy raised both fists with her thumbs up. "Let's boogie-woogie!"

Miley tucked her long blond Hannah hair up under her bike helmet. "It's time for some Hannah magic!"

Chapter Nine

When the elevator doors opened to Nicola Umberto's showroom, Miley knew it was showtime. She was Hannah Montana, superstar! She flipped her long blond hair over her shoulder and waltzed right up to the guard. Before she could say anything, he jumped up.

"You're Hannah Montana!" he exclaimed, smiling. He didn't seem so stern anymore.

Miley nodded, trying to be cool. "Muscleman is all mush for Hannah Montana,"

Jackson said to Daniella.

"That's Hannah Montana?" Daniella whispered. "Wow, I love her music."

Finally, Jackson thought. This Hannah Montana thing is actually useful. He couldn't believe he'd found a girl who was beautiful—and thought Mighty Brinito was the ultimate comic-book hero. "It just so happens that I have an extra ticket to her concert tonight," he said, feeling very cool. He sat up a bit straighter. "Are you interested in going?"

Daniella's mouth dropped open. "Those tickets have been sold out for months! I'd love to go!" Then she paused for a moment. "Wait, what about Miley? Doesn't she want the ticket?"

"Um, Miley?" Jackson said, stalling. "She . . . um . . . she's busy," he said quickly.

"Oh, that's right," Daniella said. "She mentioned something about meeting up with your dad."

Jackson let out a deep breath. "You know, it's a father-daughter thing."

"If she won't mind, then I'd be glad to go," Daniella said.

"Actually, she'd love it if you went. Trust me," Jackson said.

"Cool!" Daniella said, grinning. She looked over at the elevator doors. "I hope Miley gets back soon so she can see Hannah. I can't believe that I'm shopping at the same place as a pop star!"

Jackson watched as Muscleman knocked on the door three times. The plan was a success! He smiled at Daniella. "Believe it!"

A glamorous young woman appeared at the door. She was wearing all white, and her wavy blond hair fell to her shoulders. Muscleman spoke quickly in Italian to her.

"This is Patricia," Muscleman said to Miley. "She will take you in to meet Nicola."

Miley smiled. Before she went inside, she

looked back at Jackson and Daniella. They were both sitting on the bench watching her. As Daniella turned to whisper in Jackson's ear, Miley winked at her brother. It seemed the plan was working for everyone!

Patricia led her through a few rows of long racks filled with clothes. Miley couldn't believe all the clothes! Each fabric was more beautiful than the next! Nicola had so many different styles. Miley was so excited to be in the showroom. As she looked around, she wished that Daniella was there with her.

In the back of the room, there was a large open space. A white leather couch faced three full-length mirrors. Around the room were curtains leading to other rooms.

"*Prego*, sit," the woman said with a very strong accent. She smiled and ducked away behind one of the curtains.

Miley settled back into the soft couch. Hanging on a rack in front of her were three tops that she would love to own! One of them would be perfect for the finale tonight, she thought. She could wear her new boots, too!

"*Ciao!*" a young woman called. She rushed into the room. Her dark hair was very short and framed her small, round face. "I'm Nicola. I'm so happy to meet you!" Her green eyes were sparkling, and her cheeks were flushed. "I can't believe that Hannah Montana is here in my showroom!"

"And *I* am so happy to meet *you*!" Miley said, laughing. She stood up and shook Nicola's hand.

Nicola took Miley's hand and sat down next to her on the couch. "This is unbelievable! All the way from America? How did you hear about me?"

Miley took a good look at Nicola. She seemed young for a designer and had a very warm smile. Miley liked her right away.

"I love your work," Miley said, smiling.

"I'm here on tour, and I saw someone wearing one of your fabulous shirts."

Before Miley could continue, Patricia was back with a tray of small bottles of water. Behind her was another woman who was pushing a rack of clothes toward the couch.

"We thought you'd like to look at this selection," Nicola said.

"*Grazie*," Miley said. Now it was her turn to blush! The clothes on the rack before her were beautiful! Miley jumped up to look through the selection. Each piece was different—and so cool! Then a deep purple silk shirt caught her eye. It would be perfect with her black leggings—and of course, her new black boots. An amazing outfit for the finale!

"Ah, this would be beautiful on you," Nicola said. She noticed that the purple shirt had caught the superstar's eye. She stood next to Miley and reached for the shirt.

Holding it in her hand, she turned to her new client. "Do you want to try it on?"

"*Si!*" Miley exclaimed. She giggled and ducked behind the curtain. As she pulled the shirt on, Miley knew she had to have it. It fit her perfectly! When she walked out to the three large mirrors, Nicola and Patricia smiled.

"*Perfecto!*" they both said at the same time.

"*Grazie*," Miley said. She turned around and caught a view of herself in each of the large mirrors. "I'm going to wear this tonight!" She tossed her hair over her shoulder.

"At your concert?" Nicola asked.

"I needed a new outfit for the finale," Miley explained. "And this is perfect."

Nicola looked very pleased. "That would be a huge honor."

Miley pulled out two tickets to the Hannah Montana concert from her bag. "Please, be my guests tonight!" Miley said.

"Your show has been sold out for months," Nicola cried. "This is unbelievable!"

Miley took a step back from the mirror and faced the young designer. "Nicola, there are two Americans and their Italian friend waiting outside your showroom," she told her. "They are the real reason I'm here. They told me about you, and where to find you. The guard outside, well, he . . ." Miley chose her words carefully. "He is very strict. He wouldn't let them in."

Shaking her head, Nicola looked away. She seemed embarrassed. "I'm sorry," she said. "Tony is my cousin, and he is very protective. He is taking his security job too seriously. Of course we'll let your friends in. Any friend of Hannah Montana is a friend of ours!"

"Thank you," Miley said. "I wish that I could stay, but I have to run. This has really been fun."

Nicola clapped her hands together. "*Grazie!*" she said. "Will you really wear this tonight?"

"For sure!" Miley said. "I love it!"

"I'll make sure your friends get to come in," Nicola told her. "Again, I apologize for Tony's behavior."

As Miley headed to the door, she called over her shoulder. "You don't have to apologize to me. Please don't let them know that I told you," she added. "They are very proud."

"Ah, I understand," Nicola said. She gave Miley a kiss on each cheek. "*Ciao!*"

"*Ciao!*" Miley called as she rushed past Tony—straight into the elevator. Quickly, she glanced over at Jackson and Daniella, who were still sitting on the couch. Daniella's nose was in the *Mighty Brinito* comic book.

In the elevator, Miley removed her Hannah wig and clothes to reveal her regular

Miley clothes underneath. Just as planned, Roxy was waiting downstairs. Miley handed Roxy her Hannah wig and clothes, and the bag with her new shirt.

"See you back here in ten minutes," Roxy said. She slipped her on black helmet and zoomed off on her scooter.

Miley blew the hair off her forehead. She jumped into the elevator, anxious to get back upstairs to Nicola's showroom. When the elevator doors opened this time, Tony greeted her warmly.

"Your friends are already inside," he said. "Nicola is waiting for you."

Miley smiled. She walked into the show-room and found Jackson sitting on the white couch in front of the three mirrors. Daniella was happily sorting through a long rack of clothes. When Daniella looked up and saw Miley, she flashed a huge grin.

"Look at all these amazing clothes!" she

exclaimed. "It's like being on a fashion photo shoot. It's all so glamorous."

Miley had to agree. Nicola's showroom may not have been listed in her dad's guidebooks, but this was definitely an Italian sight that Miley was happy to see!

"I have a date tonight," Daniella whispered. She leaned in closer to Miley. "Jackson asked me to go see the Hannah Montana concert. He said that you wouldn't mind, since you have plans with your dad . . ."

Before Daniella could go on, Miley held up a cute blue top. "This would be great," she said. Daniella went to the dressing room.

"Well Jackson-o, looks like Italy's working out just fine for you," said Miley.

"What can I say?" Jackson answered. "The Italians find me irresistible."

Miley rolled her eyes. She looked at her watch. She had a concert to get to—and fast.

Chapter Ten

When the last note of the final song came to an end, Miley took her bow. The crowd went wild! Hannah Montana had been a huge hit! Maybe it was her new black leather boots, maybe it was her new Nicola Umberto shirt, or maybe it was just a good set. Whatever it was, everything had clicked into place for the concert, and Miley was feeling good. She had definitely rocked Rome! And luckily she'd gotten there in the nick of time.

* * *

*E*arly the next morning, Miley's dad walked into the living room carrying a large silver tray with several newspapers piled up high. "Roberto sent these up, along with a very large fruit platter," he said.

"Yum," Miley said, rubbing her eyes. *"Grazie!"*

Laughing, her dad sat down beside her. "Seems like you've got a large fan club here in Rome," he said. He tapped the tray of papers. "These reviews are excellent."

"Really?" Miley asked. She bolted up and grabbed the newspapers, but then quickly put them down. "They are all in Italian," she said. "What do they say? What's the review?"

"They all mention the purple shirt that you wore during the finale. I think you might have made that new designer's career!" Jackson said, poking his head into the room. "Oh, yeah, and something about how you rocked the house."

Miley giggled. "How cool! Wait till I tell Lilly!" She jumped out of bed and grabbed her phone to e-mail Lilly. To her surprise, there was already a message waiting for her. Miley read the message quickly and laughed. "Lilly says to get her a koala when we go to Australia."

Mr. Stewart gave his daughter a big hug. "Well, let's just enjoy Rome. We don't leave for Sydney till tonight. I'm very proud of you," he added. "That concert last night was really one of your best."

"Thanks, Dad," Miley said, smiling. "And don't worry, I'm all yours this morning! We can get some espresso, and I definitely want to see the inside of the Colosseum! We could even do a Hannah photo op there right before we leave."

Mr. Stewart rubbed his chin. "Hmm," he said. "That is not a bad idea, Mile. Not at all. I'll call Phillipa, our local publicist. We'll get to spend time together, and afterward you can do a quick change."

"This tour was a fantastic idea," Miley told her dad.

Jackson took a bite of a nectarine. "Hmmm, I'll say," he added. "Amazing comics, unbelievable food, and beautiful girls. I like it here."

"Did you and Daniella have fun last night?" Miley asked, hitting him playfully.

"She's a huge Hannah Montana fan!" Jackson exclaimed. "She actually knew every word to every song!"

Mr. Stewart grinned. "I bet you loved that!"

"Listen, she loves Mighty Brinito," Jackson said. "So that balances it out."

"That's great, son," Mr. Stewart said. He turned to Miley. "Why don't you hit the shower, and we'll leave in a half hour."

Jackson sat down on one of the fluffy couches with his *Mighty Brinito* comic book and an Italian-to-English dictionary.

Excited to spend the morning with her dad, Miley got ready quickly. She was off to see the sights of Rome!

A few hours later, Miley came back to the suite. She and her dad had walked all over. They'd gone to the Forum and St. Peter's Basilica. Then they'd wandered over to the Colosseum. That had been her favorite part. She'd imagined singing there in ancient Rome. Before she'd changed into her Hannah clothes for the photographers and had a photo op outside, she and her dad had their picture taken inside.

Now all Miley wanted to do was chill out. But as soon as she walked into her suite, the phone rang. It was Jackson.

"Miley!" he cried. "I'm in the lobby. Daniella is here. She really wants to talk to you!"

"I'll be right down," Miley said. As tired as

she was, Miley wanted to see her new friend before they left.

"Have you heard?" Daniella exclaimed as soon as she saw Miley. She held out several newspapers. "Everyone is talking about the Hannah Montana concert and how she wore a Nicola Umberto shirt during the finale. Now Nicola will be an incredibly popular designer! All these papers are saying she's the hottest new label. And we have two shirts from her fall line!"

"Really?" Miley said, trying not to smile.

"*Si,*" Daniella went on. "You were the one who spotted Nicola's designs. How cool to have the same style sense as a top American pop star! Hannah Montana was even wearing tall leather boots like the ones you bought the other day!"

Miley smiled. "Really? I guess we both have excellent taste!" she said.

"I wanted to give you both my e-mail

address so we can keep in touch." Nicola handed Miley and Jackson each a piece of paper. "Do you have a few minutes before you leave?" Daniella asked.

Jackson leaped forward. "Sure, what do you have in mind?"

"There is some place that I would like to show you both," Daniella explained.

Miley and Jackson followed Daniella out of the hotel. They walked a few blocks and came upon a place that Miley had seen pictures of in several of the Rome guidebooks. It was the famous Trevi Fountain. Thanks to her dad, Miley knew there was a legend that if someone threw a coin in the fountain, that person would return to Rome soon.

"Here," Daniella said. She handed her friends each a coin. "If you throw this in the fountain, you'll be sure to come back."

"And we both plan on doing that!" Jackson said. He reached out for the coin and threw it. But he was so excited, he threw the coin too high. *Bonk!* It hit a man reading a newspaper on the head. *"Scusi!"* Jackson yelled.

Daniella giggled. "Here, try again," she said, handing him another coin.

This time, Jackson wasn't taking any chances. He ran to the edge of the fountain and dropped the coin in.

Miley smirked. "Nice throw." She turned to Daniella. "Thank you for making this visit to Rome so much fun," she said.

Miley tossed her coin. It splashed into the fountain.

Miley looked around happily. She couldn't believe all of the cool things that had happened here. This might be the first stop on her world tour—but she definitely planned on returning to Rome!

Don't miss the next stop on the tour!

G'day, Sydney!

Written by M. C. King

Based on the series created by Michael Poryes and Rich Correll & Barry O'Brien

Miley Stewart is jetting off to Australia for the next stop on Hannah Montana's world tour. But when she arrives, she's shocked to hear that everyone thinks Hannah is feuding with Gemma, an Aussie teen TV star. And that's not all—it turns out Gemma is also the daughter of one of Mr. Stewart's oldest friends! Before she knows it, Miley has to get ready for a boomerang-throwing showdown between Hannah and Gemma. Luckily, Mr. Stewart has a secret weapon up his sleeve. . . .

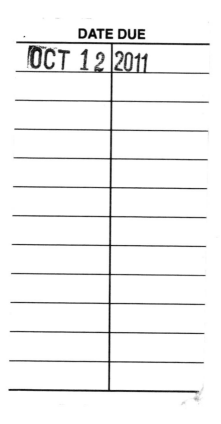

DATE DUE

OCT 12 2011